Lydia
the Reading
Fairy

by Daisy Meadows

SCHOLASTIC INC.

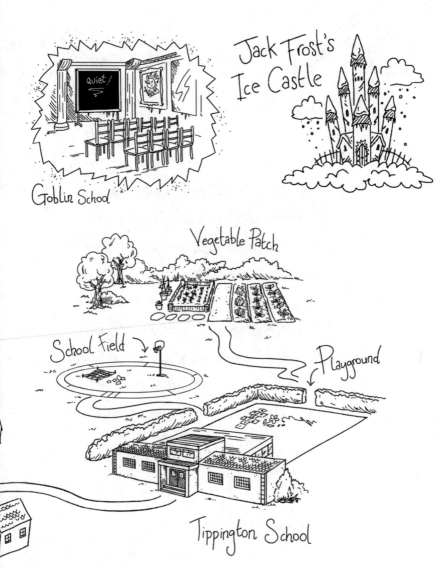

Goblin School

Jack Frost's Ice Castle

Vegetable Patch

School Field

Playground

Tippington School

It's time that pesky Lydia sees
How wonderful a school can be—
A place where goblins are always bossed,
And learn lots about the great Jack Frost.

Now her special badge of gold
Makes goblins do what they are told.
Let the silly fairy whine and wail.
My cleverness will never fail!

Contents

Backward Books   1

A Shocking School Visitor   11

A Rhyming Spell and a Reading   25

Punished!   37

Hop, Skip, and Jump   47

The Goblin School Library   59

Backward Books

"I love the smell of libraries, don't you?" said Kirsty Tate.

She took a deep breath and looked around at the bookshelves of the Tippington School library. Her best friend, Rachel Walker, smiled at her.

"I love having you here at school with me," she said. "I wish it were for longer than a week!"

It was only the third day of the new school year, but Rachel already had tons of fun with Kirsty there. She had lots of friends at Tippington School, but none was as special as her best friend. Rachel had often wished that they could go to the same school, but they lived in different towns.

Then, after a series of late-summer storms, Kirsty's school had been flooded. The builders had said that the repairs would take another week. So for five happy days, the best friends were able to go to school together at last.

In some ways, it felt like a wish come true.

The truth was, Rachel and Kirsty had shared many special times. The two friends had an extraordinary secret. From the time when they first met on Rainspell Island, they had been friends of Fairyland.

They had shared many magical adventures and met lots of different fairies. Each one had a special magic talent. Kirsty and Rachel had even visited Fairyland as the special guests of Queen Titania and King Oberon, the kind rulers of the fairy kingdom.

"I can only think of one thing more exciting than having you here with me," Rachel said.

Kirsty responded with a big smile. She knew just what her friend was thinking. What if they could help another fairy?

Before Rachel could say more, the homeroom teacher clapped his hands together to get everyone's attention.

"I want each of you to choose a book to read," said Mr. Beaker. "Then write a few sentences about what you think of the book. All the book reports will be included in the library display. The display will get the school excited for our upcoming read-a-thon."

"What kind of book should we choose?" asked Adam, one of Rachel's classmates.

"Try to pick something that you think will transport you to another world,"

said Mr. Beaker. "I love reading, and the best books are the ones where the story comes to life. The characters should seem as real to you as your best friend."

The children started to wander around the library, browsing the shelves.

"Be brave in your book choice," Mr. Beaker went on. "It might be exciting to pick something that you wouldn't normally read. Surprise yourself!"

Suddenly, there was a loud crash, and two girls jumped back from the shelves where they had been browsing. Three heavy books had almost landed on top of them.

"Please be careful," said Mr. Beaker.

"But, Mr. Beaker, they just fell off the shelf," cried one of the girls. "We didn't touch them!"

"Excuse me, I think this book is glued shut," said Adam, who was trying to look at a mystery. "I can't open it."

Rachel had just chosen a book called *The Princess in the Tower*. But when she opened it, none of the sentences made sense. She blinked a few times, wondering if her eyes were playing tricks on her. But there was definitely something very odd about the book.

"Everything is backward," she whispered to Kirsty. "Listen, this is how the story begins: 'After ever happily lived Rose Princess.' Something weird has happened in here. The books are all wrong—and I bet I know why."

Kirsty knew exactly what her best friend was thinking. They had seen weird things like this before, and it was always for the same reason: Jack Frost.

"Jack Frost must be up to his old tricks again," Kirsty guessed.

"This can't be good," Rachel replied, shaking her head.

"Jack Frost and his goblins have caused so much trouble for the fairies in the past," Kirsty said in a low voice. "I wonder what they're up to now."

Cranky Jack Frost was always making problems for the fairies. He was pesky and selfish, and usually up to no good. He liked to send his goblins to do his dirty work.

Kirsty and Rachel had often worked with the fairies to ruin Jack Frost's evil

plans, and they had tricked lots of his goblins in the process.

Rachel started to scan the room, looking for clues. Just then, the library door swung open. Two boys walked in. They let the door slam, and then strutted past the computer station. While they were wearing school uniforms, they were not Tippington School uniforms. The boys had on bright-green blazers and matching caps. The caps had extra-long bills that covered their faces.

"We're new," one of the boys said.

"We want to read books," said the other. "Cool books."

Mr. Beaker looked confused, but he forced himself to smile. "Well, you've come to the right place," he said. Then

he opened his notebook and looked at his class roster.

"Here are your names," he responded. "I don't know why I didn't see them before."

Kirsty and Rachel exchanged glances. "It's the third day of school," Rachel commented. "Why are they just showing up now?"

Both of the girls gave the new boys a closer look, and then stared at each other in surprise.

A Shocking School Visitor

The girls realized something at the exact same time. The two new boys in their class were not really boys at all! Their disguises had fooled Mr. Beaker and the other children, but Kirsty and Rachel were very good at spotting goblins. The two new students had already disappeared in the back of the library.

"We should find those goblins and figure out what they're doing," Rachel whispered.

Kirsty nodded. Mr. Beaker wasn't watching them—he was too busy trying to open Adam's book. The girls made their way toward the back of the library, where the lights were dim and all the least-borrowed books were kept. Not many students were looking in this section, but the girls could hear loud, screechy voices. They looked at each other.

"Goblins," they said together.

They peeked around a tall bookshelf and saw

the two goblins sitting cross-legged on the floor.

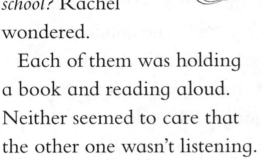

What are they doing here, in my school? Rachel wondered.

Each of them was holding a book and reading aloud. Neither seemed to care that the other one wasn't listening.

"Once upon a time there was a grumpy troll who liked to eat princes and princesses," the first goblin read in a loud voice. "But there weren't enough princes and princesses to fill him up. So he decided to go on vacation with his best friend, a handsome goblin."

"Milly, Tilly, and Gilly were sisters," the second goblin read in an equally loud voice. "They were human beings, so of course they were very silly and annoying. One day, a happy little goblin was stealing some apples from an orchard. At that very moment, the sisters decided to poke their noses in." The goblin paused and looked at his friend. "This book is so much better than the crummy one Jack Frost was reading," he said.

"This one is even better," the other goblin bragged.

"They love the sound of their own voices, don't they!" said Rachel.

"Yes," said Kirsty with a frown, "and it seems like those stories have been changed—they don't sound right at all."

Just then, they heard footsteps coming up

from behind them. They whirled around and saw Mr. Beaker coming their way. When he spotted the girls and heard the voices, he stopped. Rachel and Kirsty thought that he might scold the goblins for being so loud, but he just smiled.

"I'm glad to hear someone in the class is enjoying their books," he said. "I don't know what's gone wrong, but library time doesn't seem to be very much fun today."

"Do you want us to ask those boys to be quiet, Mr. Beaker?" Kirsty asked.

The teacher shook his head.

"It's nice to hear that they're so enthusiastic," he said. "I don't mind a little bit of noise now and then."

As he walked away, the girls exchanged a surprised glance.

"I suppose the main thing is that they're not causing any trouble," said Rachel. "For now!" But she did wonder why the goblins were in the human world. They belonged in Fairyland!

"Look at that bookshelf over there," said Kirsty in a hushed voice.

She pointed to a bookshelf in the corner. One of the shelves seemed to be gleaming with a faint light, and the girls hurried toward it.

"The light must be coming from one of the books on this shelf," said Rachel. "I'll bet you know what I'm thinking."

"Of course," replied Kirsty. "It looks just like a fairy glow. I hope you're right."

They searched through the books that were on the shelf until they found one that was shimmering with a bright golden light.

"This must be the one," said Rachel, taking it down from the shelf. She opened it, and out fluttered a charming fairy! Her black hair was tied in a thick side braid, and she was wearing flowery shorts with a pink sweater.

"Hello, Rachel! Hello, Kirsty!" said the fairy.

"You know who we are?" Kirsty asked.

"Of course! You are two of the fairies' favorite friends. You are always so happy to offer your help." The fairy had a very sweet smile, but she sounded anxious. "Speaking of which," she continued, "I could really use your help. Right now. Queen Titania told me that I could find you here."

"Queen Titania?" Kirsty said. "I hope everyone's okay in Fairyland."

"Yes," Rachel agreed, sounding concerned. "Please tell us how we can help."

The fairy bit her lip. "I'm getting ahead of myself. First of all, my name is Lydia. I'm the Reading Fairy."

Both the girls said it was nice to meet her. Then Lydia quickly told her tale.

"As the Reading Fairy, I have a special badge. It helps keep reading books fun and magical," Lydia explained. "But yesterday, the horrible Jack Frost stole it."

"That's awful," the girls replied together.

"The weird part is that Jack Frost took it because he's starting his own school. He's the head teacher, and he's making the students learn all about him!"

"That *is* odd," agreed Rachel.

"The worst part is that it's causing problems in Fairyland," Lydia said. "All the books in the fairy school are blank. The words just disappeared!"

"The books in this library are messed up, too," Kirsty replied. "We have to fix it. We have a book report due today!"

"My magic badge affects things in Fairyland and the human world. We can make things right. We just have to find my magic gold star badge. Then we need to get it back to the library at the Fairyland school." Lydia glanced up and down the rows of bookshelves.

"I'm sure it must be around here somewhere," she said. "Please, will you help me find it? Children all over the world have stopped enjoying reading, and it's all because of Jack Frost."

"Of course we'll help," said Rachel. "Lydia, there is something you should know. There are two goblins in this library right now."

"Are there really?" Lydia asked. "Queen Titania mentioned that two of Jack Frost's students escaped. They were fed up with his school, and they took my magic badge when they left."

"Do you think these are the same goblins?" asked Kirsty.

"I'll bet they are," Lydia replied. "Where did you see them?"

"They are just over there. They are reading out loud," Rachel said.

"If they are enjoying their books, they probably have my magic badge," Lydia explained.

Kirsty realized something. The goblins were the only ones who had found books they could read. "They have to have it," she said.

"Let's go and tell them to give your badge back," Rachel insisted.

Lydia nodded at once.

"Jack Frost makes me nervous, but I'm not scared of goblins," she said. "Let's go and talk to them right now."

She hid in Rachel's pocket and then the girls walked toward the tall bookshelf where the goblins were reading. But before they got there, Kirsty grabbed Rachel's arm.

"Look!" she whispered. "Between those books!"

In a gap between some books on a
shelf, the girls could see an ice-blue robe
and the tip of a graduation hat. Holding
their breaths, they tiptoed up to the shelf
and peeked through to the other side.
Then Rachel and Kirsty grasped each
other's hands in shock.

Jack Frost was in their school!

A Rhyming Spell and a Reading

Jack Frost was sneaking down the row of shelves, heading toward the goblins. They hadn't noticed him because they were so interested in their books. They were still reading aloud.

"The grumpy troll and the handsome goblin snowboarded down the snowy

mountain," the first goblin read at the top of his lungs. "Everyone gasped. They had never seen such amazing skill and speed. The goblin and troll were more graceful than Olympic athletes and faster than fairies."

"The goblin found a really cool hiding place for the apples," bellowed the second goblin. "But Milly, Tilly, and Gilly cheated and spied on him, and they took the apples back to the orchard. So the goblin locked them

in an ice castle for a hundred years, and
that served them right."

"BOO!" shouted Jack Frost, leaping
out in front of them.

Frightened, the goblins jumped to their
feet, dropping the books on the floor.
Jack Frost walked slowly toward them,
and they backed away until they ran
into a bookshelf.

"I've come to take back my magic badge," he said. "You goblins are going to give it to me—right now!"

He pulled a blue book out from under his robe. Rachel and Kirsty could see the title clearly, because it was written in shiny silver letters: *Fantastic Jack Frost: The Story of My Life.*

"This is the best book in the world," he said. "I want every single goblin in my school to hear the story, but not one of them is paying attention and it's all your fault!"

He was shaking with rage. The goblins held their breaths, and their knees started to knock together.

"W–w–what can we d–d–do, Your Iciness?" asked the first goblin. The second goblin opened his mouth to speak but couldn't get any words to come out, so he gave a curtsy instead. "Give me the badge!" Jack Frost roared.

Trembling, the first goblin put his hand into his pocket and pulled out a shiny golden badge.

"That's it!" said
Lydia. "My badge!
My beautiful
badge!"

But before
the girls
could do
anything,
Jack Frost had
snatched the badge and disappeared in a
crack of blue lightning! The two goblins
had disappeared with him.

"Quick, use your magic!" Rachel
begged Lydia. "We have to catch up
with Jack Frost! He must have gone back
to Fairyland."

Lydia fluttered out of Rachel's pocket
and hovered in front of them, holding

up her wand and speaking the words
of a spell.

"*Follow Jack Frost without delay*
To find the gold badge he stole away.
Whether in sunshine or in snow,
Take us where he chose to go."

With a whooshing sound, a ribbon
of sparkling fairy dust wound
around the girls,
wrapping them
in magic.
They closed
their eyes,
and their
shoulder
blades tingled
as glittery

wings appeared. They heard the tinkle of faraway bells, and then felt a blast of ice-cold air. When they opened their eyes, they were standing inside a very different kind of library.

Icicles were hanging from the shelves, and there were patches of ice on the threadbare carpet. But the strangest thing was that every book in the library was exactly the same, row after row. The girls gazed at thousands of thick blue spines, all with the same title written in silver letters: *Fantastic Jack Frost: The Story of My Life.* They were inside the library of Jack Frost's Ice Castle!

Lydia and the girls were standing between two rows of bookshelves. Before they could say a word, they saw Jack Frost striding across the front of the

library. There was a crowd of goblin students sitting on the carpet in front of him.

"Hide!" said Kirsty with a gasp.

They fluttered over to hide behind a bookshelf at the back of the library, close to the door.

"I thought Jack Frost said that the goblins weren't paying attention," Rachel whispered. "They all look very well behaved to me."

"There's a good reason for that," said Lydia, looking serious. "Look at what he's wearing on his robe."

The girls peeked through the shelves and saw Lydia's special badge glittering on Jack Frost's robe. The golden star had a magical glow.

"That's why the goblins are being so good," said Kirsty.

They watched as Jack opened a copy of his book and started to read.

"Chapter One," he began. "The fairies have always caused trouble for me, and their sense of right and wrong is always getting in my way. One day, I decided

that enough was enough. My brilliant
brain instantly thought of a fantastic
plan to stop them, once and for all."

Jack Frost was a terrible reader. He
was so boring! He didn't change the tone
of his voice at all. Instead, he droned on
and on. Soon, the girls were yawning,
but the goblins kept listening as if the
story was the most wonderful thing that
they had ever heard.

"We need to do something to stop him
before we all fall asleep," said Lydia.

"We have to get the badge back,"
Rachel declared. "But *how*?"

Punished!

Rachel looked around and noticed a bell hanging on a hook by the library door. She tapped Kirsty on the shoulder and pointed at the bell.

"I'll bet Jack Frost rings that bell when it's time for a break," she said. "It would be much easier to get the badge away from him if the goblins were playing outside. Lydia, I have a plan. But first, Kirsty and I need to look like goblins."

Lydia smiled and held up her wand.

"Let my spell hide both these faces.
Cast away all human graces.
Disguise my friends as goblins green,
And let no fairy wings be seen."

The girls felt a creepy,
tickling feeling as
their clothes
changed into
green goblin
uniforms. Their
noses and ears
grew long and
pointy, and their
hair shrank
away until they
were bald.

"Rachel, you look funny!" said Kirsty with a giggle.

"You do, too!" said Rachel, giving her a hug. "I'm glad it's only for a short while."

They made their way over to the library door, hoping that Jack Frost wouldn't see them. Luckily, he was still busy reading all about himself. They could hear his booming voice.

"That was when I generously decided to give some goblins the chance to work with me," he declared. "I visited the goblin village and chose the best of the best. The chosen goblins kissed both my hands in thanks."

"This is definitely not a good story," said Rachel.

She reached up and rang the bell as

loudly as she could. At the front of the library, Jack Frost jumped in surprise and immediately stopped reading. The goblins scrambled to their feet and stampeded toward the door.

"Let me out!" Kirsty heard one of them mutter.

"That story! I couldn't take another word," whispered another.

"But I couldn't stop listening," said a third. "Something was forcing me to be good. It was awful." Rachel recognized the last two. They were the goblins that had been in the Tippington School library.

The group of goblins pushed and shoved one another aside, trying to reach the door first. Rachel and Kirsty had to run to get out of their way. In the confusion, they ran in the wrong direction—straight into the arms of Jack Frost!

Jack Frost pinched one of Kirsty's goblin ears between his thumb and his forefinger. He did the same to Rachel, and he frowned at them both.

"I saw what you two did!" he snapped. "You rang the recess bell too early! You interrupted the amazing story of my life! You're going to be punished for that!"

"We're very sorry," said Kirsty, trying to whimper like a real goblin. "Please don't punish us!"

But Jack Frost was furious, and he wouldn't let go of their ears.

"You will miss out on recess," he said. "You will have to sit in my office and work. Come on!"

Rachel and Kirsty exchanged a hopeful glance. Maybe this would be their chance to get Lydia's badge back!

Pulling Rachel and Kirsty along by the ears, Jack Frost marched them out of the library and along a dim, damp hallway to his office.

By twisting her head around, Rachel could see that Lydia was hovering behind them in the shadows. The little fairy gave an encouraging nod and quickly crossed her fingers.

Jack Frost kicked the door open and shoved the girls inside. Then he marched around to the chair behind his desk and sat down. Lydia had just enough time to

slip inside the room before the door banged shut. Kirsty saw her hide behind a large potted plant. It contained a very droopy-looking cactus.

"You two are going to learn that when I'm talking, you should be listening," said Jack Frost. "You should have been paying attention in class." He stared them down as he drummed his long fingers on his desk. "As punishment, I want you each to write a whole page about why *Fantastic Jack Frost: The Story of My Life* is the best book ever."

"Oh, thank you!" exclaimed Kirsty,

much to Rachel's surprise. Jack Frost
looked shocked, too. "That's a wonderful
assignment," Kirsty went on. "I could talk
for days about your book. It is so exciting!
You have lived such an interesting life."

A smile flickered across Jack Frost's
face. It raised the edges of his grumpy
mouth. Rachel suddenly guessed Kirsty's
idea. If they could distract Jack Frost,
Lydia might be able to unpin the badge
from his robe.

Hop, Skip, and Jump

"I can't wait to finish reading your amazing book," Rachel said.

"It's a real page-turner," said Jack Frost, stroking his spiky beard.

"Will you sign some copies of your book for us?" asked Kirsty, clasping her hands together.

"Very well, very well," said Jack Frost.

He sounded almost kind. There was a big pile of his books on the table, and he opened one and began to sign his name with a leaky fountain pen. Lydia swooped down, ducked under his arm and started to undo the pin on the badge. But just as he finished signing the second book, the fountain pen squirted a blob of ink onto his robe. He glanced down—and saw Lydia trying to take the badge!

"A FAIRY IN MY OFFICE?" bellowed Jack Frost. "How dare you, you winged pest! I'll put you in detention! I'll give you a year's worth of homework! I'll make you take tests every day! COME HERE!"

He tried to trap Lydia between his hands, but she zoomed away and flew out through the open window. Jack Frost hurled himself over the windowsill and ran after her. His long robe flapped behind him as he ran.

"They're heading for the playground,"
cried Rachel. "Come on—we have to
stop him from catching Lydia!"

She and Kirsty climbed out of the
window, too, and followed Jack Frost
toward the icy playground. He was still
yelling at Lydia, but now he was also
panting, because he was so out of shape.
Rachel and Kirsty finally reached the
playground. The ice was so slippery, they
almost skidded into some goblins playing
hopscotch.

"Watch it!" the goblins yelled rudely.

The girls wanted to say sorry, but they
knew that a real goblin would never be
that polite! They stuck out their tongues
and the other goblins did the same.

"*YOWCH!*" squealed a tall goblin.

A warty goblin had landed on his foot. But as he hopped around, clutching his toes, he tripped over a goblin with a jump rope. They both fell flat on their faces, tangled in the rope.

Rachel nudged Kirsty's arm.

"Those clumsy goblins just gave
me an idea," she said. "Maybe
our big goblin feet can trip up
Jack Frost."

"Let's try it!" Kirsty said eagerly.

They raced after Jack Frost, who
was sprinting around the playground,
grabbing at the fairy. Lydia fluttered
right in front of him. She zigzagged
left and right. It was hard for the girls
to keep up with them. At last, they
were close enough to Jack Frost's
trailing robe.

"Ready . . . JUMP!" shouted Rachel.

They sprang through the air and
landed on the hem of the long, blue
robe with their big feet. Their weight
yanked the robe off, and Jack Frost

staggered sideways.
He lost his
footing and
tumbled
into a
snowy
sandbox.

Lydia
made a
big loop
in the air and
swooped down to the robe. She quickly
unpinned the gold badge before Jack
Frost could get to his feet. She then
zoomed out of his reach.

"Give it back!" screamed Jack Frost,
stamping his feet and waving his fists in
the air. "You tricky little fairy! Give me
my badge!"

"It's *my* badge," said Lydia in her gentle voice. "Thanks to my friends, I have it back. Now people all over the world will be able to enjoy reading again."

As she spoke, Rachel and Kirsty's disguises melted away. Once they had their wings back, they fluttered upward to join Lydia. Jack Frost turned a very strange purple color when he realized he had been tricked. He snatched up his robe, stomped over to the outside bell, and rang it angrily.

"Everyone inside—NOW!" he
bellowed. "If I can't have any fun, then
neither can you!"

The goblins grumbled and stayed on
the playground. None of them wanted
to listen to another reading from Jack
Frost's book. But Jack Frost looked
especially angry, so one by one they all
shuffled back into school. Lydia, Kirsty,
and Rachel hovered in the air and
watched them.

"Are we
going to
take the
badge back
to the fairy
school library
now?" Kirsty

asked, after the last goblin had gone inside.

"Well . . ." said Lydia. "Maybe it's silly, but I actually feel kind of sorry for Jack Frost. After all, he went to the trouble of writing a book, and now no one wants to read it."

The girls understood how the kind little fairy was feeling.

"Maybe there's something we can do to help," said Rachel. "Should we go back into the library and find out?"

The others nodded at once, and together they flew back into the goblin school. There was a terrible noise coming from the library. Goblins were squawking, shrieking, and thundering around like a herd of elephants. Jack Frost was sitting at a desk with his head

in his hands. Lydia looked around and folded her arms.

"The trouble is that these students are bored," she said. "I can't blame them. What good is a library where every book is the same? I have an idea!"

The Goblin School Library

Lydia flew up near the center of the ceiling and waved her wand in a wide circle. As a shower of fairy dust rained down on the library shelves, she recited a spell:

"Transform this room into a place
Of wondrous books and reading space.
Books you read til lights go out.

Books you tell your friends about.
Princesses young and witches old,
Adventures wild and heroes bold.
Books that make you laugh out loud,
Real-life tales to make you proud.
Stories that can break your heart.
Stories that are works of art.
Poems, plays, and novels, too.
Fill these dreary shelves anew!"

As she spoke, the endless copies of *Fantastic Jack Frost: The Story of My Life* began to change. One by one, a colorful selection of books appeared, in all shapes and sizes. As the goblins started to notice and talk about it, Jack Frost looked up. He groaned when he saw all the copies of his book disappearing.

Rachel and Kirsty flew over and

landed on the desk in front of Jack Frost.
He scowled at them.

"What do you want?" he demanded.

"We'd like to have the copies of your
book that you signed for us earlier," said
Rachel, trying to sound brave.

Jack Frost's mouth fell open. He stared
at them for a moment. Then he stood up
and hurried off to get the books. While
he was gone, the goblins
grew quieter and
quieter. One by
one, they were
discovering
exciting books
and settling
down to read
them. Even the
two goblins who

had been in the library at Rachel's school were reading quietly. By the time Jack Frost returned, the goblins were completely spellbound by their different books.

"There," said Jack Frost, shoving the copies of his book at Rachel and Kirsty.

But he didn't sound nearly as grumpy as usual!

Just then, a very small goblin tapped him on the shoulder.

"I thought you might like this book, sir," said the goblin in a shaky voice.

He held out a copy of *The Snow Queen*. Jack Frost grabbed it and read the back cover.

"Aha!" he exclaimed. "She sounds like my kind of character!"

He sat down and started reading. With a smile, Lydia landed on the desk next to Rachel and Kirsty.

"You've been wonderful," she said. "Thank you from the bottom of my heart. But now it's time for us all to go home."

The girls kissed her good-bye. Then, a flurry of magic sparkles lifted them into the air. Brushing fairy

dust from their eyes, they blinked . . . and found themselves sitting in the Tippington School Library. Just like magic!

Everyone was busy writing about the books they had chosen. Kirsty and Rachel looked down and smiled. There was a copy of *Fantastic Jack Frost: The Story of My Life* in front of each of them.

"I think it's time to write a book report!" Rachel whispered.

In a short while, Mr. Beaker cleared
his throat.

"All right, everyone," he said. "I'd like
to hear what you thought about your
books. Let's start with Rachel Walker."

Rachel and Kirsty stood up together.

"We chose the same book," Rachel
explained. "It's all
about someone
called Fantastic
Jack Frost.
I liked
this book
because
the main
character
tries to be scary,

but sometimes he's very funny
without even knowing it."

"I like the way all the characters come to life in the book," Kirsty added. "You could almost believe that Fairyland and all the various fairies really do exist."

Rachel shared a secret smile with her best friend.

"Well, it sounds like a really interesting book," said Mr. Beaker. "I've never heard of it before, but you've made me want to read it. I think that all these reports will get the whole school excited for the read-a-thon."

Kirsty and Rachel sat down again as Adam started to read his book report.

"In all the excitement, I forgot about the read-a-thon," Rachel whispered. "I can't wait to discover many more exciting books."

Kirsty nodded, and smiled. "I hope all

the fairies and goblins back in Fairyland
get to read new books, too."

"I'm sure they will," Rachel said.
"Because we know one thing for certain.
All fairy stories end happily ever after!"

Don't miss any of Rachel and Kirsty's
other fairy adventures!
Check out this magical sneak peek of

Carly
the School Fairy!

Competition
Countdown

Rachel Walker strolled over to the grand
doors of Tippington Town Hall and
peered outside. There were buses pulling
up and lots of people milling around, but
no sign of the very special person she was
looking for, her best friend, Kirsty Tate!

Rachel's school was taking part in an exciting competition. Four schools from different parts of the country were competing in two different events; a spelling bee was going to be held today at Tippington Town Hall and a science fair was to take place at the Science Museum tomorrow.

Rachel was part of the Tippington School spelling bee team, but the *most* exciting thing was that Kirsty's school was also taking part in the competition.

"Rachel! Over here!" called Kirsty. Rachel turned around and there was Kirsty!

The girls split off from the main group of students and teachers in the hall, and made their way toward a side entrance. As they strolled along, something in one

of the trophy cases caught Kirsty's eye. "Rachel, what *is* that?" she asked, stepping closer.

"It's just the light shining on the Tippington in Bloom cup, isn't it?" replied Rachel, still walking toward the auditorium.

"I think it's something even more special than that!" whispered Kirsty happily, tugging on Rachel's arm. Rachel stopped suddenly. There, sitting on the edge of a shiny trophy surrounded by a magical glow, was a beautiful little fairy!

RAINBOW magic™

Which Magical Fairies Have You Met?

- ☐ The Rainbow Fairies
- ☐ The Weather Fairies
- ☐ The Jewel Fairies
- ☐ The Pet Fairies
- ☐ The Dance Fairies
- ☐ The Music Fairies
- ☐ The Sports Fairies
- ☐ The Party Fairies
- ☐ The Ocean Fairies
- ☐ The Night Fairies
- ☐ The Magical Animal Fairies
- ☐ The Princess Fairies
- ☐ The Superstar Fairies
- ☐ The Fashion Fairies
- ☐ The Sugar & Spice Fairies
- ☐ The Earth Fairies
- ☐ The Magical Crafts Fairies
- ☐ The Baby Animal Rescue Fairies

■ SCHOLASTIC

Find all of your favorite fairy friends at
scholastic.com/rainbowmagic

HIT entertainment

RMFAIRY12